THE MYSTERIOUS DEATH
ON THE
UNDERGROUND RAILWAY

BY

BARONESS EMMUSKA ORCZY

British Library Cataloguing-in-Publication Data
A catalogue record for this book is available from the
British Library

CONTENTS

CONTENTS

BARONESS EMMA ORCZY

Baroness Emma Magdolna Rozália Mária Jozefa Borbála "Emmuska" Orczy de Orczi was born in Heves County, Hungary, in 1865. Her family moved between Budapest, Brussels and Paris, before settling in London in 1880, where Orczy attended West London School of Art and then Heatherley's School of Fine Art. It was here that she met her future husband, a young illustrator named Montague MacLean Barstow. The two of them married in 1894.

Orczy and Barstow were not well-off, and Orczy started to work with her husband as a translator and an illustrator to supplement his low wage. In 1899, the same year that they had their first and only child, Orczy produced her first novel, *The Emperor's Candlesticks*. However, real success came in 1903, when she and Barstow wrote a play based on one of her short stories, set during the French Revolution. *The Scarlet Pimpernel* was not an instant success, but following a rewritten last act and an opening in the West End, the play went on to run for four years in London, playing more than 2,000 performances. It broke many stage records, was translated and produced in various other countries, and underwent several revivals.

Orczy went on to write over a dozen sequels to *The Scarlet*

Pimpernel, as well as a good amount of popular mystery fiction and adventure romances, some of which feature early examples of female lead detectives. Her money worries vanished; in fact, Orczy became so well-off that she was able to buy an estate in Monte Carlo. During the First World War, she worked hard to recruit female volunteers for active service. She also lived through the Second World War, before dying in Henley-on-Thames of old age.

THE MYSTERIOUS DEATH ON THE UNDERGROUND RAILWAY

BARONESS EMMUSKA ORCZY

It was all very well for Mr Richard Frobisher (of the *London Mail*) to cut up rough about it. Polly did not altogether blame him.

She liked him all the better for that frank outburst of manlike ill-temper which, after all said and done, was only a very flattering form of masculine jealousy.

Moreover, Polly distinctly felt guilty about the whole thing. She had promised to meet Dickie – that is Mr Richard Frobisher – at two o'clock sharp outside the Palace Theatre, because she wanted to go to a Maud Allan matinée, and because he naturally wished to go with her.

But at two o'clock sharp she was still in Norfolk Street, Strand, inside an ABC shop, sipping cold coffee opposite a grotesque old man who was fiddling with a bit of string.

How could she be expected to remember Maud Allan or the Palace Theatre, or Dickie himself for a matter of that?

3

The man in the corner had begun to talk of that mysterious death on the Underground railway, and Polly had lost count of time, of place, and circumstance.

She had gone to lunch quite early, for she was looking forward to the matinée at the Palace. The old scarecrow was sitting in his accustomed place when she came into the ABC shop, but he had made no remark all the time that the young girl was munching her scone and butter. She was just busy thinking how rude he was not even to have said 'Good morning', when an abrupt remark from him caused her to look up.

'Will you be good enough,' he said suddenly, 'to give me a description of the man who sat next to you just now, while you were having your cup of coffee and scone.'

Involuntarily Polly turned her head towards the distant door, through which a man in a light overcoat was even now quickly passing. That man had certainly sat at the next table to hers, when she first sat down to her coffee and scone: he had finished his luncheon – whatever it was – a moment ago, had paid at the desk and gone out. The incident did not appear to Polly as being of the slightest consequence.

Therefore she did not reply to the rude old man, but shrugged her shoulders, and called to the waitress to bring her bill.

'Do you know if he was tall or short, dark or fair?'

continued the man in the corner, seemingly not the least disconcerted by the young girl's indifference. 'Can you tell me at all what he was like?'

'Of course I can,' rejoined Polly impatiently, 'but I don't see that my description of one of the customers of an ABC shop can have the slightest importance.'

He was silent for a minute, while his nervous fingers fumbled about in his capacious pockets in search of the inevitable piece of string. When he had found this necessary 'adjunct to thought', he viewed the young girl again through his half-closed lids, and added maliciously:

'But supposing it were of paramount importance that you should give an accurate description of a man who sat next to you for half an hour today, how would you proceed?'

'I should say that he was of medium height—'

'Five foot eight, nine, or ten?' he interrupted quietly.

'How can one tell to an inch or two?' rejoined Polly crossly. 'He was between colours.'

'What's that?' he enquired blandly.

'Neither fair nor dark – his nose—'

'Well, what was his nose like? Will you sketch it?'

'I am not an artist. His nose was fairly straight – his eyes—'

'Were neither dark nor light – his hair had the same striking peculiarity – he was neither short nor tall – his nose was neither aquiline nor snub—' he recapitulated sarcastically.

'No,' she retorted; 'he was just ordinary-looking.'

'Would you know him again – say tomorrow, and among a number of other men who were "neither tall nor short, dark nor fair, aquiline nor snub-nosed", etc.?'

'I don't know – I might – he was certainly not striking enough to be specially remembered.'

'Exactly,' he said, while he leant forward excitedly, for all the world like a Jack-in-the-box let loose. 'Precisely; and you are a journalist – call yourself one, at least – and it should be part of your business to notice and describe people. I don't mean only the wonderful personage with the clear Saxon features, the fine blue eyes, the noble brow and classic face, but the ordinary person – the person who represents ninety out of every hundred of his own kind – the average Englishman, say, of the middle classes, who is neither very tall nor very short, who wears a moustache which is neither fair nor dark, but which masks his mouth, and a top hat which hides the shape of his head and brow, a man, in fact, who dresses like hundreds of his fellow-creatures, moves like them, speaks like them, has no peculiarity.

'Try to describe *him*, to recognise him, say a week hence, among his other eighty-nine doubles; worse still, to swear his life away, if he happened to be implicated in some crime, wherein *your* recognition of him would place the halter round his neck.

'Try that, I say, and having utterly failed you will more readily understand how one of the greatest scoundrels unhung is still at large, and why the mystery on the Underground railway was never cleared up.

'I think it was the only time in my life that I was seriously tempted to give the police the benefit of my own views upon the matter. You see, though I admire the brute for his cleverness, I did not see that his being unpunished could possibly benefit anyone.

'In these days of tubes and motor traction of all kinds, the old-fashioned "best, cheapest, and quickest route to City and West End" is often deserted, and the good old Metropolitan railway carriages cannot at any time be said to be overcrowded. Anyway, when that particular train steamed into Aldgate at about four p.m. on March eighteenth last, the first-class carriages were all but empty.

'The guard marched up and down the platform looking into all the carriages to see if anyone had left a halfpenny evening paper behind for him, and opening the door of one of the first-class compartments, he noticed a lady sitting in the further corner, with her head turned away towards the window, evidently oblivious of the fact that on this line Aldgate is the terminal station.

' "Where are you for, lady?" he said.

'The lady did not move, and the guard stepped into the carriage, thinking that perhaps the lady was asleep. He touched her arm lightly and looked into her face. In his own poetic language, he was "struck all of a 'eap". In the glassy eyes, the ashen colour of the cheeks, the rigidity of the head, there was the unmistakable look of death.

'Hastily the guard, having carefully locked the carriage door, summoned a couple of porters, and sent one of them off to the police station, and the other in search of the stationmaster.

'Fortunately at this time of day the up platform is not very crowded, all the traffic tending westward in the afternoon. It was only when an inspector and two police constables, accompanied by a detective in plain clothes and a medical officer, appeared upon the scene, and stood round a first-class railway compartment, that a few idlers realised that something unusual had occurred, and crowded round, eager and curious.

'Thus it was that the later editions of the evening papers, under the sensational heading, "Mysterious Suicide on the Underground Railway", had already an account of the extraordinary event. The medical officer had very soon come to the decision that the guard had not been mistaken, and that life was indeed extinct.

'The lady was young, and must have been very pretty

before the look of fright and horror had so terribly distorted her features. She was very elegantly dressed, and the more frivolous papers were able to give their feminine readers a detailed account of the unfortunate woman's gown, her shoes, hat, and gloves.

'It appears that one of the latter, the one on the right hand, was partly off, leaving the thumb and wrist bare. That hand held a small satchel, which the police opened, with a view to the possible identification of the deceased, but which was found to contain only a little loose silver, some smelling-salts, and a small empty bottle, which was handed over to the medical officer for purposes of analysis.

'It was the presence of that small bottle which had caused the report to circulate freely that the mysterious case on the Underground railway was one of suicide. Certain it was that neither about the lady's person, nor in the appearance of the railway carriage, was there the slightest sign of struggle or even of resistance. Only the look in the poor woman's eyes spoke of sudden terror, of the rapid vision of an unexpected and violent death, which probably only lasted an infinitesimal fraction of a second, but which had left its indelible mark upon the face, otherwise so placid and so still.

'The body of the deceased was conveyed to the mortuary. So far, of course, not a soul had been able to identify her, or to throw the slightest light upon the mystery which hung around her death.

'Against that, quite a crowd of idlers – genuinely interested or not – obtained admission to view the body, on the pretext of having lost or mislaid a relative or a friend. At about eight-thirty p.m. a young man, very well dressed, drove up to the station in a hansom, and sent in his card to the superintendent. It was Mr Hazeldene, shipping agent, of 11, Crown Lane, EC, and No. 19, Addison Row, Kensington.

'The young man looked in a pitiable state of mental distress; his hand clutched nervously a copy of the *St James's Gazette* which contained the fatal news. He said very little to the superintendent except that a person who was very dear to him had not returned home that evening.

'He had not felt really anxious until half an hour ago, when suddenly he thought of looking at his paper. The description of the deceased lady, though vague, had terribly alarmed him. He had jumped into a hansom, and now begged permission to view the body, in order that his worst fears might be allayed.

'You know what followed, of course,' continued the man in the corner, 'the grief of the young man was truly pitiable. In the woman lying there in a public mortuary before him, Mr Hazeldene had recognised his wife.

'I am waxing melodramatic,' said the man in the corner, who looked up at Polly with a mild and gentle smile, while his nervous fingers vainly endeavoured to add another knot on the scrappy bit of string with which he was continually playing, 'and I fear that the whole story savours of the penny novelette, but you must admit, and no doubt you remember, that it was an intensely pathetic and truly dramatic moment.

'The unfortunate young husband of the deceased lady was not much worried with questions that night. As a matter of fact, he was not in a fit condition to make any coherent statement. It was at the coroner's inquest on the following day that certain facts came to light, which for the time being seemed to clear up the mystery surrounding Mrs Hazeldene's death, only to plunge that same mystery, later on, into denser gloom than before.

'The first witness at the inquest was, of course, Mr Hazeldene himself. I think everyone's sympathy went out to the young man as he stood before the coroner and tried to throw what light he could upon the mystery. He was well dressed, as he had been the day before, but he looked terribly ill and worried, and no doubt the fact that he had not shaved gave his face a careworn and neglected air.

'It appears that he and the deceased had been married some six years or so, and that they had always been happy in their married life. They had no children. Mrs Hazeldene seemed to enjoy the best of health till lately, when she had

had a slight attack of influenza, in which Dr Arthur Jones had attended her. The doctor was present at this moment, and would no doubt explain to the coroner and the jury whether he thought that Mrs Hazeldene had the slightest tendency to heart disease, which might have had a sudden and fatal ending.

'The coroner was, of course, very considerate to the bereaved husband. He tried by circumlocution to get at the point he wanted, namely, Mrs Hazeldene's mental condition lately. Mr Hazeldene seemed loath to talk about this. No doubt he had been warned as to the existence of the small bottle found in his wife's satchel.

' "It certainly did seem to me at times," he at last reluctantly admitted, "that my wife did not seem quite herself. She used to be very gay and bright, and lately I often saw her in the evening sitting, as if brooding over some matters, which evidently she did not care to communicate to me."

'Still the coroner insisted, and suggested the small bottle.

' "I know, I know," replied the young man, with a short, heavy sigh. "You mean – the question of suicide – I cannot understand it at all – it seems so sudden and so terrible – she certainly had seemed listless and troubled lately – but only at times – and yesterday morning, when I went to business, she appeared quite herself again, and I suggested that we should go to the opera in the evening. She was delighted, I know, and told me she would do some shopping, and pay a few calls in the afternoon.

' "Do you know at all where she intended to go when she got into the Underground railway?"

' "Well, not with certainty. You see, she may have meant to get out at Baker Street, and go down to Bond Street to do her shopping. Then again, she sometimes goes to a shop in St Paul's Churchyard, in which case she would take a ticket to Aldersgate Street; but I cannot say."

' "Now, Mr Hazeldene," said the coroner at last very kindly, "will you try to tell me if there was anything in Mrs Hazeldene's life which you know of, and which might in some measure explain the cause of the distressed state of mind, which you yourself had noticed? Did there exist any financial difficulty which might have preyed upon Mrs Hazeldene's mind; was there any friend – to whose intercourse with Mrs Hazeldene – you – er – at any time took exception? In fact," added the coroner, as if thankful that he had got over an unpleasant moment, "can you give me the slightest indication which would tend to confirm the suspicion that the unfortunate lady, in a moment of mental anxiety or derangement, may have wished to take her own life?"

'There was silence in the court for a few moments. Mr Hazeldene seemed to everyone there present to be labouring under some terrible moral doubt. He looked very pale and wretched, and twice attempted to speak before he at last said in scarcely audible tones:

' "No; there were no financial difficulties of any sort. My wife had an independent fortune of her own – and she had no extravagant tastes—"

' "Nor any friend you at any time objected to?" insisted the coroner.

' "Nor any friend, I – at any time objected to," stammered the unfortunate young man, evidently speaking with an effort.

'I was present at the inquest,' resumed the man in the corner, after he had drunk a glass of milk and ordered another, 'and I can assure you that the most obtuse person there plainly realised that Mr Hazeldene was telling a lie. It was pretty plain to the meanest intelligence that the unfortunate lady had not fallen into a state of morbid dejection for nothing, and that perhaps there existed a third person who could throw more light on her strange and sudden death than the unhappy, bereaved young widower.

'That the death was more mysterious even than it had at first appeared became very soon apparent. You read the case at the time, no doubt, and must remember the excitement in the public mind caused by the evidence of the two doctors. Dr Arthur Jones, the lady's usual medical man, who had attended her in a last very slight illness, and who had seen her in a professional capacity fairly recently, declared most emphatically that Mrs Hazeldene suffered from no organic complaint which could possibly have been the cause of sudden death. Moreover, he had assisted Mr Andrew Thornton, the district medical officer, in making a post-mortem examination, and together they had come to the conclusion that death was due to the action of prussic acid, which had caused instantaneous failure of the heart, but how the drug had been administered neither he nor his colleague were at present able to state.

' "Do I understand, then, Dr Jones, that the deceased died, poisoned with prussic acid?"

' "Such is my opinion," replied the doctor.

' "Did the bottle found in her satchel contain prussic acid?"

' "It had contained some at one time, certainly."

' "In your opinion, then, the lady caused her own death by taking a dose of that drug?"

' "Pardon me, I never suggested such a thing; the lady died poisoned by the drug, but how the drug was administered we cannot say. By injection of some sort, certainly. The drug certainly was not swallowed; there was not a vestige of it in the stomach."

' "Yes," added the doctor in reply to another question from the coroner, "death had probably followed the injection in this case almost immediately; say within a couple of minutes, or perhaps three. It was quite possible that the body would not have more than one quick and sudden convulsion, perhaps not that; death in such cases is absolutely sudden and crushing."

'I don't think that at the time anyone in the room realised how important the doctor's statement was, a statement which, by the way, was confirmed in all its details by the district medical officer, who had conducted the postmortem. Mrs Hazeldene had died suddenly from an injection of prussic acid, administered no one knew how or when. She had been travelling in a first-class railway carriage at a busy time of the day. That young and elegant woman must have had singular nerve and coolness to go through the process of a self-inflicted injection of a deadly poison in the presence of perhaps two or three other persons.

'Mind you, when I say that no one there realised the importance of the doctor's statement at that moment, I am wrong; there were three persons, who fully understood at once the gravity of the situation, and the astounding development which the case was beginning to assume.

'Of course, I should have put myself out of the question,' added the weird old man, with that inimitable self-conceit peculiar to himself. 'I guessed then and there in a moment where the police were going wrong, and where they would go on going wrong until the mysterious death on the Underground railway had sunk into oblivion, together with the other cases which they mismanage from time to time.

'I said there were three persons who understood the gravity of the two doctors' statements – the other two were, firstly, the detective who had originally examined the railway carriage, a young man of energy and plenty of misguided intelligence, the other was Mr Hazeldene.

'At this point the interesting element of the whole story was first introduced into the proceedings, and this was done through the humble channel of Emma Funnel, Mrs Hazeldene's maid, who, as far as was known then, was the last person who had seen the unfortunate lady alive and had spoken to her.

' "Mrs Hazeldene lunched at home," explained Emma, who was shy, and spoke almost in a whisper; "she seemed well and cheerful. She went out at about half-past three, and told me she was going to Spence's, in St Paul's Churchyard, to try on her new tailor-made gown. Mrs Hazeldene had meant to go there in the morning, but was prevented as Mr Errington called."

' "Mr Errington?" asked the coroner casually. "Who is Mr Errington?"

'But this Emma found difficult to explain. Mr Errington was – Mr Errington, that's all.

' "Mr Errington was a friend of the family. He lived in a flat in the Albert Mansions. He very often came to Addison Row, and generally stayed late."

'Pressed still further with questions, Emma at last stated that latterly Mrs Hazeldene had been to the theatre several times with Mr Errington, and that on those nights the master looked very gloomy, and was very cross.

'Recalled, the young widower was strangely reticent. He gave forth his answers very grudgingly, and the coroner was evidently absolutely satisfied with himself at the marvellous way in which, after a quarter of an hour of firm yet very kind questionings, he had elicited from the witness what information he wanted.

'Mr Errington was a friend of his wife. He was a gentleman of means, and seemed to have a great deal of time at his command. He himself did not particularly care about Mr Errington, but he certainly had never made any observations to his wife on the subject.

' "But who is Mr Errington?" repeated the coroner once more. "What does he do? What is his business or profession?"

' "He has no business or profession."

' "What is his occupation, then?"

' "He has no special occupation. He has ample private means. But he has a great and very absorbing hobby."

' "What is that?"

' "He spends all his time in chemical experiments, and is, I believe, as an amateur, a very distinguished toxicologist." '

'Did you ever see Mr Errington, the gentleman so closely connected with the mysterious death on the Underground railway?' asked the man in the corner as he placed one or two of his little snap-shot photos before Miss Polly Burton.

'There he is, to the very life. Fairly good-looking, a pleasant face enough, but ordinary, absolutely ordinary.

'It was this absence of any peculiarity which very nearly, but not quite, placed the halter round Mr Errington's neck.

'But I am going too fast, and you will lose the thread.

'The public, of course, never heard how it actually came about that Mr Errington, the wealthy bachelor of Albert Mansions, of the Grosvenor, and other young dandies' clubs, one fine day found himself before the magistrate at Bow Street, charged with being concerned in the death of Mary Beatrice Hazeldene, late of No. 19, Addison Row.

'I can assure you both press and public were literally flabbergasted. You see, Mr Errington was a well-known and very popular member of a certain smart section of London society. He was a constant visitor at the opera, the racecourse, the Park, and the Carlton, he had a great many friends, and there was consequently quite a large attendance at the police court that morning.

'What had transpired was this:

'After the very scrappy bits of evidence which came to light at the inquest, two gentlemen bethought themselves that perhaps they had some duty to perform towards the State and the public generally. Accordingly they had come forward, offering to throw what light they could upon the mysterious affair on the Underground railway.

'The police naturally felt that their information, such as it was, came rather late in the day, but as it proved of paramount importance, and the two gentlemen, moreover, were of undoubtedly good position in the world, they were thankful for what they could get, and acted accordingly; they accordingly brought Mr Errington up before the magistrate on a charge of murder.

'The accused looked pale and worried when I first caught sight of him in the court that day, which was not to be wondered at, considering the terrible position in which he found himself.

'He had been arrested at Marseilles, where he was preparing to start for Colombo. I don't think he realised how terrible his position really was until later in the proceedings, when all the evidence relating to the arrest had been heard, and Emma Funnel had repeated her statement as to Mr Errington's call at 19, Addison Row, in the morning, and Mrs Hazeldene starting off for St Paul's Churchyard at three-thirty in the afternoon.

'Mr Hazeldene had nothing to add to the statements he had made at the coroner's inquest. He had last seen his wife alive on the morning of the fatal day. She had seemed very well and cheerful.

'I think everyone present understood that he was trying to say as little as possible that could in any way couple his deceased wife's name with that of the accused.

'And yet, from the servant's evidence, it undoubtedly leaked out that Mrs Hazeldene, who was young, pretty, and evidently fond of admiration, had once or twice annoyed her husband by her somewhat open, yet perfectly innocent, flirtation with Mr Errington.

'I think everyone was most agreeably impressed by the widower's moderate and dignified attitude. You will see his photo there, among this bundle. That is just how he appeared in court. In deep black, of course, but without any sign of ostentation in his mourning. He had allowed his beard to grow lately, and wore it closely cut in a point.

'After his evidence, the sensation of the day occurred. A tall, dark-haired man, with the word "City" written metaphorically all over him, had kissed the book, and was waiting to tell the truth, and nothing but the truth.

'He gave his name as Andrew Campbell, head of the firm of Campbell & Co., brokers, of Throgmorton Street.

'In the afternoon of March eighteenth Mr Campbell, travelling on the Underground railway, had noticed a very pretty woman in the same carriage as himself. She had asked him if she was in the right train for Aldersgate. Mr Campbell replied in the affirmative, and then buried himself in the Stock Exchange quotations of his evening paper.

'At Gower Street, a gentleman in a tweed suit and bowler hat got into the carriage, and took a seat opposite the lady. She seemed very much astonished at seeing him, but Mr Andrew Campbell did not recollect the exact words she said.

'The two talked to one another a good deal, and certainly the lady appeared animated and cheerful. Witness took no notice of them; he was very much engrossed in some calculations, and finally got out at Farringdon Street. He noticed that the man in the tweed suit also got out close behind him, having shaken hands with the lady, and said in a pleasant way: "Au revoir! Don't be late tonight." Mr Campbell did not hear the lady's reply, and soon lost sight of the man in the crowd.

'Everyone was on tenter-hooks, and eagerly waiting for the palpitating moment when witness would describe and identify the man who last had seen and spoken to the unfortunate woman, within five minutes probably of her strange and unaccountable death.

'Personally I knew what was coming before the Scots stockbroker spoke.

'I could have jotted down the graphic and lifelike description he would give of a probable murderer. It would have fitted equally well the man who sat and had luncheon at this table just now; it would certainly have described five out of every ten young Englishmen you know.

'The individual was of medium height, he wore a moustache which was not very fair nor yet very dark, his hair was between colours. He wore a bowler hat, and a tweed suit – and – and – that was all – Mr Campbell might perhaps know him again, but then again, he might not – he was not paying much attention – the gentleman was sitting on the same side of the carriage as himself – and he had his hat on all the time. He himself was busy with his newspaper – yes – he might know him again – but he really could not say.

'Mr Andrew Campbell's evidence was not worth very much, you will say. No, it was not in itself, and would not have justified any arrest were it not for the additional statements made by Mr James Verner, manager of Messrs Rodney & Co., colour printers.

'Mr Verner is a personal friend of Mr Andrew Campbell, and it appears that at Farringdon Street, where he was waiting for his train, he saw Mr Campbell get out of a first-class railway carriage. Mr Verner spoke to him for a second, and then, just as the train was moving off, he stepped into the same compartment which had just been vacated by the stockbroker and the man in the tweed suit. He vaguely recollects a lady sitting in the opposite corner to his own, with her face turned away from him, apparently asleep, but he paid no special attention to her. He was like nearly all businessmen when they are travelling – engrossed in his paper. Presently a special quotation interested him; he wished to make a note of it, took out a pencil from his waistcoat pocket, and seeing a clean piece of paste-board on the floor, he picked it up, and scribbled on it the memorandum, which he wished to keep. He then slipped the card into his pocket-book.

' "It was only two or three days later," added Mr Verner in the midst of breathless silence, "that I had occasion to refer to these same notes again.

' "In the meanwhile the papers had been full of the mysterious death on the Underground railway, and the names of those connected with it were pretty familiar to me. It was, therefore, with much astonishment that on looking at the paste-board which I had casually picked up in the railway carriage I saw the name on it, Frank Errington."

'There was no doubt that the sensation in court was almost unprecedented. Never since the days of the Fenchurch Street mystery, and the trial of Smethurst, had I seen so much excitement. Mind you, I was not excited – I knew by now every detail of that crime as if I had committed it myself. In fact, I could not have done it better, although I have been a student of crime for many years now. Many people there – his friends, mostly – believed that Errington was doomed. I think he thought so, too, for I could see that his face was terribly white, and he now and then passed his tongue over his lips, as if they were parched.

'You see he was in the awful dilemma – a perfectly natural one, by the way – of being absolutely incapable of *proving* an alibi. The crime – if crime there was – had been committed three weeks ago. A man about town like Mr Frank Errington might remember that he spent certain hours of a special afternoon at his club, or in the Park, but it is very doubtful in nine cases out of ten if he can find a friend who could positively swear as to having seem him there. No! no! Mr Errington was in a tight corner, and he knew it. You see, there were – besides the evidence – two or three circumstances which did not improve matters for him. His hobby in the direction of toxicology, to begin with. The police had found in his room every description of poisonous susbtances, including prussic acid.

'Then, again, that journey to Marseilles, the start for Colombo, was, though perfectly innocent, a very unfortunate one. Mr Errington had gone on an aimless voyage, but the public thought that he had fled, terrified at his own crime. Sir Arthur Inglewood, however, here again displayed his marvellous skill on behalf of his client by the masterly way in which he literally turned all the witnesses for the Crown inside out.

'Having first got Mr Andrew Campbell to state positively that in the accused he certainly did *not* recognise the man in the tweed suit, the eminent lawyer, after twenty minutes' cross-examination, had so completely upset the stockbroker's equanimity that it is very likely he would not have recognised his own office-boy.

'But through all his flurry and all his annoyance Mr Andrew Campbell remained very sure of one thing; namely, that the lady was alive and cheerful, and talking pleasantly with the man in the tweed suit up to the moment when the latter, having shaken hands with her, left her with a pleasant "Au revoir! Don't be late tonight." He had heard neither scream nor struggle, and in his opinion, if the individual in the tweed suit had administered a dose of poison to his companion, it must have been with her own knowledge and free will; and the lady in the train most emphatically neither looked nor spoke like a woman prepared for a sudden and violent death.

'Mr James Verner, against that, swore equally positively that he had stood in full view of the carriage door from the moment that Mr Campbell got out until he himself stepped into the compartment, that there was no one else in that carriage between Farringdon Street and Aldgate, and that the lady, to the best of his belief, had made no movement during the whole of that journey.

'No; Frank Errington was *not* committed for trial on the capital charge,' said the man in the corner with one of his sardonic smiles, 'thanks to the cleverness of Sir Arthur Inglewood, his lawyer. He absolutely denied his identity with the man in the tweed suit, and swore he had not seen Mrs Hazeldene since eleven o'clock in the morning of that fatal day. There was no *proof* that he had; moreover, according to Mr Campbell's opinion, the man in the tweed suit was in all probability not the murderer. Common sense would not admit that a woman could have a deadly poison injected into her without her knowledge, while chatting pleasantly to her murderer.

'Mr Errington lives abroad now. He is about to marry. I don't think any of his real friends for a moment believed that he committed the dastardly crime. The police think they know better. They do know this much, that it could not have been a case of suicide, that if the man who undoubtedly travelled with Mrs Hazeldene on that fatal afternoon had no crime upon his conscience he would long ago have come forward and thrown what light he could upon the mystery.

'As to who that man was, the police in their blindness have not the faintest doubt. Under the unshakeable belief that Errington is guilty they have spent the last few months in unceasing labour to try and find further and stronger proofs of his guilt. But they won't find them, because there are none. There are no positive proofs against the actual murderer, for he was one of those clever blackguards who think of everything, foresee every eventuality, who know human nature well, and can foretell exactly what evidence will be brought against them, and act accordingly.

'This blackguard from the first kept the figure, the personality, of Frank Errington before his mind. Frank Errington was the dust which the scoundrel threw metaphorically in the eyes of the police, and you must admit that he succeeded in blinding them – to the extent even of making them entirely forget the one simple little sentence, overheard by Mr Andrew Campbell, and which was, of course, the clue to the whole thing – the only slip the cunning rogue made – "Au revoir! Don't be late tonight." Mrs Hazeldene was going that night to the opera with her husband—

'You are astonished?' he added with a shrug of the shoulders, 'you do not see the tragedy yet, as I have seen it before me all along. The frivolous young wife, the flirtation with the friend? – all a blind, all pretence. I took the trouble which the police should have taken immediately, of finding out something about the finances of the Hazeldene *ménage*. Money is in nine cases out of ten the keynote to a crime.

'I found that the will of Mary Beatrice Hazeldene had been proved by the husband, her sole executor, the estate being sworn at fifteen thousand pounds. I found out, moreover, that Mr Edward Sholto Hazeldene was a poor shipper's clerk when he married the daughter of a wealthy builder in Kensington – and then I made note of the fact that the disconsolate widower had allowed his beard to grow since the death of his wife.

'There's no doubt that he was a clever rogue,' added the strange creature, leaning excitedly over the table, and peering into Polly's face. 'Do you know how that deadly poison was injected into the poor woman's system? By the simplest of all means, one known to every scoundrel in southern Europe. A ring – yes! a ring, which has a tiny hollow needle capable of holding a sufficient quantity of prussic acid to have killed two persons instead of one. The man in the tweed suit shook hands with his fair companion – probably she hardly felt the prick, not sufficiently in any case to make her utter a scream. And, mind you, the scoundrel had every facility, through his friendship with Mr Errington, of procuring what poison he required, not to mention his friend's visiting card. We cannot gauge how many months ago he began to try and copy Frank

Errington in his style of dress, the cut of his moustache, his general appearance, making the change probably so gradual, that no one in his own entourage would notice it. He selected for his model a man his own height and build, with the same coloured hair.'

'But there was the terrible risk of being identified by his fellow-traveller in the Underground,' suggested Polly.

'Yes, there certainly was that risk; he chose to take it, and he was wise. He reckoned that several days would in any case elapse before that person, who, by the way, was a businessman absorbed in his newspaper, would actually see him again. The great secret of successful crime is to study human nature,' added the man in the corner, as he began looking for his hat and coat. 'Edward Hazeldene knew it well.'

'But the ring?'

'He may have bought that when he was on his honeymoon,' he suggested with a grim chuckle; 'the tragedy was not planned in a week, it may have taken years to mature. But you will own that there goes a frightful scoundrel unhung. I have left you his photograph as he was a year ago, and as he is now. You will see he has shaved his beard again, but also his moustache. I fancy he is a friend now of Mr Andrew Campbell.'

He left Miss Polly Burton wondering, not knowing what

to believe.

And that is why she missed her appointment with Mr Richard Frobisher (of the *London Mail*) to go and see Maud Allan dance at the Palace Theatre that afternoon.